Prince of the
Potty

ISBN: 978-1-60169-077-7

Published by innovativeKids®
A division of innovative USA®, Inc.
50 Washington St.
Norwalk, CT 06854
iKids is a registered trademark in Canada and Australia.

www.innovativekids.com

Printed in China
5 7 9 10 8 6 4

I'm a big boy now!

I can run.

I can kick.

I can climb.

I can swing.

I'm getting stronger and smarter every day. Mom and Dad call me their little prince.

But I still wear a diaper. I pee and poop in my diaper. That makes it heavy and very smelly!

I don't think I like that squishy, wet feeling anymore.

I think about using
the potty.

My dad uses the potty.

My grandpa
uses the potty.

Even my friend,
Max, uses the potty.

Today, Mom and Dad brought home a big boy potty, just for me!

Someday I will sit on that royal potty, and I will do my business. When I'm done, I won't forget to wash my hands!

Mom and Dad said that when I feel pee or poop coming, I should sit on the potty.

Mom takes off my diaper, and I try sitting on the potty.

I sit, and I wait.
And I wait.

I stand up and look into the potty.

Nothing.

A little while later, Mom asks me to try again. This time I try reading my book while sitting on the potty.

Finally, something happens!

I did it! I did it!
I made pee in the potty!
I made poop in the potty!

Mom and Dad are very happy.
I am very happy, too.

Mom and Dad say I'm ready for
big boy underwear.

I think about wearing underwear.

My dad wears
underwear.

My grandpa
wears underwear.

Even my friend,
Max, wears underwear.

Now I wear underwear, too!

When I need to use the potty . . .

I pull down my pants and underwear.

I go pee and poop, and then I wipe myself.

I pull my underwear and pants back up.

And then, I wash my hands!

Uh oh! I had an accident.

Mom says sometimes we have accidents, and that's okay.

Next time I get that feeling, I will remember to rush to the potty.

Now I'm very good at using my potty! Mom and Dad say I'm their big boy prince.

And I say . . .

I am Prince of the Potty!

A Note to Parents

Every child is unique, and every child learns to use the potty when he or she is ready. The key to successful potty training is a no-pressure environment where your child believes he is in control. Reading about using the potty and talking with your child are wonderful, non-threatening ways to introduce the concept to your growing boy and encourage him to become "Prince of the Potty."

Is your child ready? Ask yourself these questions:

- Does he seem interested in the potty chair, the toilet, or wearing underwear?

- Can he understand and follow basic directions?

- Does your child stay dry for periods of two or more hours during the day?

- Does he wake from naps dry?

- Is he uncomfortable in wet or dirty diapers?

- Is your child beginning to tell you through words or facial expressions when he needs to go?

Potty training success relies on emotional and physical readiness, not a specific age. If you answered yes to most of the questions above, your child may be ready. If you answered mostly no, you may want to wait. If you start potty training too early, it may take even longer.

Roll out the red carpet!

When you decide it's time to start potty training, set your little prince up for success! Be sure to keep a positive attitude and a sense of humor!

Get the equipment ready. Decide whether you will use a toilet or potty chair. Encourage your child to sit on the potty chair—with or without a diaper. You might empty the contents of a dirty diaper into the toilet or potty chair to show its purpose. It's also a good idea to let your child see family members of the same sex using the toilet.

Make potty breaks part of your day. Encourage your child to sit on the toilet or potty chair without a diaper at various times throughout the day. This is a great time to read a book or talk with him. Remember to offer praise for trying, even if nothing happens!

Consider incentives. Reinforcing your child's efforts on the potty with stickers on a chart, a trip to the park, or an extra bedtime story may be effective. Regardless of the specific incentives you use, remember to continually use verbal praise, even if a trip to the toilet isn't successful.

Be consistent. Once you establish a routine for the potty, follow it on a daily basis, and make sure that all of your child's caregivers follow it, too.

Accidents happen. Treat mistakes lightly. Accidents will happen—especially when your child is upset or tired. Remember to stay calm and reassure your child that it's okay. Keep an extra change of clothes on hand, just in case.

5 Royal Tips
for Becoming
Prince of the Potty!

1. Help your favorite stuffed animal go potty!

Sit your favorite stuffed animal on a pretend toilet, explaining "he or she is going pee in the potty." Put underwear on your stuffed animal, and applaud him or her for going potty!

2. Read on the potty!

You've probably seen Mom or Dad or your big brother or sister reading on the potty. Now it's your turn. Bring your favorite book to look at on the potty, and wait for the pee feeling to come. Reading on the potty is relaxing and fun!

3. Think of a special word or signal!

Now that you are getting to be a big boy, you will start to feel that pee or poop feeling coming. Think of a special word or signal that you can use to let Mom or Dad know that you are ready to sit on the potty. This special word or signal can be your very own top secret way to tell Mom or Dad "it's time!"

4. Buy some cool underwear!

Guess what? If you are starting to use the potty, you are ready to go shopping for big boy underwear. You will have a blast picking out awesome underwear that have your favorite characters or colors on them.

5. Say goodbye to your diapers!

You will love the feeling of being clean and dry in your new, cool underwear. Have a farewell ceremony to say goodbye to your diapers. You are a big boy now!

Celebrate!